Witch＊Wendy

Books by Alex Gutteridge

Witch Wendy

1. Cats and Hats
2. Broom Broom!
3. Cat Tricks

Witch★Wendy

Cats and Hats

Alex Gutteridge

Illustrated by Annabel Hudson

MACMILLAN CHILDREN'S BOOKS

First published 2002 by Macmillan Children's Books Ltd
a division of Macmillan Publishers Limited
20 New Wharf Road, London N1 9RR
Basingstoke and Oxford
www.panmacmillan.com

Associated companies throughout the world

ISBN 0 330 39850 4

1 3 5 7 9 8 6 4 2

A CIP catalogue record for this book is available from
the British Library.

Typeset by Macmillan Publishers Limited
Printed and bound in Great Britain by Mackays of Chatham plc, Kent

For Christopher, Nicholas and Emily

Chapter One

Witch Wendy was fed up. It had rained and rained for nights and nights. Everything was covered in mud: her cat Snowflake, her cloak and her hat.

She looked in the mirror. The hat was dirty. It was crumpled and it didn't stand up straight like a witch's hat should.

The point flopped down in front of her eyes. Even when she wore her special flying glasses, she couldn't see properly. This made riding the broomstick a big problem.

Last month Wendy had crashed into a tree; last week she had landed in a pond; and last night she had careered into all the other witches and caused a horrible pile-up. They were very cross with her, but there was nothing new about that.

"Somehow," Wendy said to Snowflake, "I need to get a new hat. Perhaps I'll try the hat spell again."

"PLEASE NO!" Snowflake miaowed loudly. "No more horrible hat tricks!" He checked his watch. "If we don't hurry we'll be late for the picnic in the park and Witch Rosemary will turn us both into frogs again."

Wendy opened the front door. The broomstick was parked outside. Snowflake fixed the picnic basket in the middle and he jumped on the back. The rain had stopped but the sky was very black and there was no hint of the moon.

"You're a clever cat, Snowflake," said Wendy, "and you can see better in the dark than I can. You drive the broomstick tonight."

"I'll have to sit at the front then," said Snowflake.

"Oh no," Wendy said. "You can't do that. It's against the Flyway Code.

Cats must always perch at the back.
We'll fly the broomstick backwards!"

"Are cats allowed to fly broomsticks?"
asked Snowflake.

"Well, no," grinned Wendy. "It'll be
our secret."

"Don't you think Witch
Rosemary will smell a
bat if we don't crash
as usual?" muttered
Snowflake.

But Wendy wasn't listening. She was trying very hard to get the Friday night flying spell right first time.

Broomstick, Broomstick, let's be quick,
we're off to the park for a witches' picnic.
Backwards, backwards, off we go,
come on broomstick,
don't be slow!"

Snowflake strapped on his crash helmet and tightened up his seat belt.

Wendy fixed on her flying glasses and waved her wand.

"Here we go again," Snowflake murmured as the broomstick zoomed down the garden path towards take-off.

Chapter Two

"YES!" squealed Wendy, bouncing up and down. "We did it first time."

"Will you please sit still," growled Snowflake. "You'll break the broomstick."

"Sorry," said Wendy, "I'll try to be good."

So the witch faced forwards, the broomstick flew backwards and Snowflake began to enjoy himself. Once or twice he peeped behind him to check Wendy was behaving.

Soon they heard sneaky laughter and rude noises in the distance.

"Watch out! Here comes Witch Wendy and her horrible hat," a voice cackled through the clouds.

"Here comes Witch Rosemary and her horrible cat," muttered Snowflake.

Witch Rosemary glided into view, her hat as tall and straight as a church spire.

"Not found the right hat spell yet, I see?" smirked Rosemary.

"I've nearly got it," lied Wendy, lifting her hat up so she could see the other witches.

"She's talking through her hat!" Witch Harriet jeered. "She shouldn't be allowed out dressed like that."

"Are you sure you can see properly?" asked Witch Primrose.

"Of course I can," said Wendy. "I'm wearing my flying glasses."

"Hmm," Witch Rosemary murmured. "I suppose you can come with us to the park, but BE CAREFUL."

"It's my turn first on the swings this week," Wendy shouted after them as Rosemary, Primrose and Harriet raced away at top speed. "Let's go faster, Snowflake. We'll soon catch them."

"But there are witches all over the place," said Snowflake as lots of shadowy figures filled the sky. "If we go any faster we'll crash."

Wendy wasn't listening.

"Broomstick, broomstick, make it

snappy, if you want this witch to be happy," she chanted.

The broomstick picked up speed and Snowflake put his paws over his eyes.

"Oh, my fearful fur," Snowflake moaned.

"Trust me," said Wendy. "I know what I'm doing."

"I've heard that before," Snowflake groaned.

"I know a short cut to the park," squealed Wendy. "We'll get there before them. Turn left, Snowflake."

Snowflake peeped through one paw.

"I don't think that's a good idea," he shouted.

"Snowflake, who's in charge here?" Wendy wriggled around on the broomstick.

Snowflake sighed and turned the broomstick to the left – straight into a scuffle of squabbling witches.

There was a loud whining noise and the broomstick went into a dive.

Wendy wailed as they headed towards the ground and Snowflake was so scared he thought his fur would turn from black to white. They crashed into a deep, dark,

muddy hole at the side of the road.

"Oops!" gulped Snowflake. "Sorry!"

"It's not your fault," said Wendy. "It's mine. I should send back my witch's licence. I'm hopeless."

"No you're not," said Snowflake.

"Yes I am," said Wendy. "I can't make rude noises like other witches."

"But I can make bad smells," said Snowflake, "especially when I've had a tin of sardines for tea."

"I can't stop frogs croaking," said the witch.

"But you've got a wonderful magic potion for sore throats," said Snowflake.

"And worst of all I can't see because I haven't got a proper hat," she sobbed.

"But you do have a wonderful cat," said Snowflake and he licked her chin.

Witch Wendy climbed out of the hole and sat on the grass verge with her head in her hands. Snowflake scrambled out after her and looked around.

"Can you see what I see?" he asked. "Or has that bump on the head affected my eyes?"

Wendy looked up. She blinked. She jumped to her feet and did a little dance. She gave Snowflake a huge hug. There, at the side of the road was a long row of witch's hats.

Chapter Three

Wendy picked up one of the hats and tried it on.

"What do you think?" she asked Snowflake.

"Well," he replied, "it's not as black as your old hat, and it's not as shiny, and it does have a sort of bobble on the top, but apart from that it's purrfect."

"I'll have it," giggled Wendy. "What a bit of luck." Suddenly she looked serious. "You don't think all these hats belong to somebody do you, Snowflake?"

"No," said Snowflake shaking his head, "they probably fell off the back of a broomstick."

"In that case," said the witch, "I might as well take all of them. It's always useful to have a few spare hats."

She gathered up all the hats, stacked them one on top of the other and balanced them on her head.

They hauled the slimy broomstick out of the deep hole and climbed aboard.

"Wait a minute," said Wendy just as Snowflake was ready to take off.

She hopped off the broomstick and hooked her old hat out of the hole with her wand. She placed it carefully at the side of the road.

"There," she said, looking very pleased with herself. "I think that looks just right."

Wendy climbed into bed just as dawn was breaking.

"I can't wait to see what Rosemary is going to say about my new hat," she giggled. "It's so unusual with that bobble on the top. Don't you think she'll be jealous, Snowflake?"

Snowflake snuggled down in his basket and closed his eyes.

"I think she'll be spellbound," he murmured.

Chapter Four

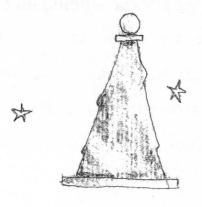

The next night was a full moon. For once Wendy couldn't wait to set off for Saturday night flying practice.

She sat up straight and tall in her new hat and enjoyed watching the twinkling stars and the feel of the cool air as it stroked her face. The broomstick didn't bump or jolt or stall once. She felt like a new witch.

She made a perfect landing on top of the bus stop where they always met.

"We're the first here," she smiled. "That'll be two surprises for them!"

"I don't know whether Rosemary is the sort of witch who likes surprises," said Snowflake.

Wendy straightened the hat on her head as Rosemary, Harriet and Primrose whizzed into view. The three witches braked suddenly and skidded into one another in front of the bus stop. Witch Rosemary scanned Wendy from top to toe.

"Where did you get that hat?" she screeched. Her green skin turned violet in the moonlight and her yellow eyes glowed red at the rims.

"How did you manage that? You can't even make a decent smell let alone a designer hat spell."

"Do you like it?" Wendy smiled.

"I want one!" Rosemary pranced up and down angrily. "Tell me how you did it."

"It's a secret," said Snowflake.

Witch Rosemary screamed like a hyena. Coalface, her cat, spat like a snake. Then Rosemary rummaged in her handbag and got out her purse.

"I'll buy that one off you. However much you want – name your price."

Wendy shook her head.

"This one's mine. But if you really want one . . ."

"I want one too," pleaded Primrose.

"And me," added Harriet.

"Twenty pounds," snarled Rosemary,

waving the money in front of her.

"Each?" queried Snowflake.

Rosemary, Primrose and Harriet nodded so hard their warts wobbled.

"I'm not sure . . ." said Wendy.

"Done," said Snowflake, whisking the money out of the witches' hands. "We'll bring the hats tomorrow night."

Flying practice went like a dream.

Wendy sprinted around church spires. She hurtled over high trees and she didn't tangle with telephone wires once. Rosemary, Primrose and Harriet went home early in a sulk.

But Wendy and Snowflake stayed out

looping the loop until the sun started to lighten the inky sky.

Later, as they snuggled up on the sofa, half asleep, Wendy whispered in Snowflake's ear.

"With a new hat my spells will be—"

"—enchanting," murmured Snowflake.

"And my broomstick racing will be—"

"—record-breaking," murmured
Snowflake.

"And it's all happened like—"

"—like magic?" murmured
Snowflake.

"Yes!" said Witch Wendy. "Just
like magic."

Chapter Five

Witch Rosemary was very pleased with her new hat. She studied her reflection in a puddle. She smiled, a horrible, crooked smile that showed rows of black and yellow rotting teeth.

"I think it suits me better than you," she said to Wendy.

"I'm glad you like it," said Wendy.

"Oh, I do," snarled Rosemary. "I'm very happy and tonight's witch-hunt in the woods is going to be the best one we've had for ages. We'll catch voles and toads and spiders by the sackful."

"Yippee!" yelled Primrose and Harriet

as they collected their new hats. "That sounds spooky."

"Sounds tasty to me," miaowed Nightshade, Primrose's cat, as he spread flying ointment on Primrose's broomstick.

"Sounds mouth-watering to me," Coalface called, licking his lips.

"Sounds lovely to me," sang Sable,

Witch Harriet's cat. "What do you think, Snowflake?"

Snowflake sighed from the pads of his paws to the ends of his ears. He blushed from the roots of his fur to the tips of his whiskers.

Sable lounged on her purple velvet cushion at the back of Harriet's broomstick and gazed at him with bluebell coloured eyes.

"Lovely," Snowflake replied. But he didn't mean the voles and toads and spiders.

"Hold on to your hats," screamed Rosemary as she rose into the air, spun the broomstick around three times and sped off deep into the countryside.

Snowflake closed his eyes and clung on with all his claws as Wendy darted after her.

The witches were so happy with their new hats they dribbled, burped and sang very badly all the way to the Woeful Wood.

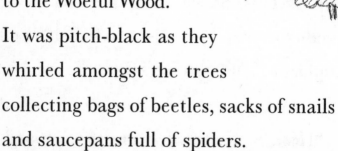

It was pitch-black as they whirled amongst the trees collecting bags of beetles, sacks of snails and saucepans full of spiders.

There was a crack of thunder overhead

and a flash of lightening filtered through
the trees.

"Here comes the delicious downpour,"
cackled Rosemary.

Huge drops of water began to splash to the ground.

"On to the pond for a toad hunt!" she cried, pointing the way with a flick of her gnarled fingers.

By the time they reached the edge of the wood the rain was teeming down. Wendy pulled her hat further down over her face and wiped her muddy hands on her cloak. She looked at the mud for a moment, puzzled. Then she looked at Rosemary, Primrose and Harriet.

The rain was washing their new hats clean. As the mud ran over the brims and on to their clothes, the hats changed to red and white, topped with an orange plastic bobble.

"What's happening to our hats?" wailed Harriet.

"Oh dear," gulped Snowflake as Wendy

watched, horrified. "I think it's time to go home. Fast."

Wendy twizzled the broomstick around and scooted for safety.

"Wendy, you wimp of a witch," roared Rosemary as she wiped her muddy hands all over Sable. "Come back here. Come and explain why our new hats have turned into traffic cones!"

Chapter Six

Witch Rosemary was in a rage. She kicked her traffic cone across Wendy's garden and hammered on the front door. Primrose and Harriet rattled at the windows and the three cats caterwauled down the chimney.

"You've gone too far this time," Rosemary screeched.

"It was a mistake," sobbed Wendy through the letter box. "You know I get in a muddle sometimes."

"You're so irritating I should turn you into a wasp," shouted Rosemary.

Snowflake opened the door a crack.

"Can we do a deal?" he asked, waving

three twenty-pound notes under Rosemary's hooked nose. "You'll get your money back if you don't make any mean magic."

Rosemary hissed like the sound of the wind whipping down a long tunnel.

She stretched out an ugly hand, grabbed the money and clambered on to her broomstick.

"You've got off lightly this time, Wendy," she called as she collected Coalface from the roof. Then she jammed Harriet and Primrose's hats over the chimney pot, sending smoke swirling back into the house.

"Oh, Snowflake," coughed Wendy. "I can't go around wearing a traffic cone for a hat. What am I going to do?"

The next night Snowflake took Wendy to look for her old hat. It was very foggy and they could hardly find their way around.

Finally, they found the right place, but the hole had been filled in and there was no sign of Wendy's old hat. She took the traffic cone off her head and scowled at it.

"I need a proper hat," she wailed. "What sort of a witch doesn't have a hat?"

She threw the cone down in a temper. As it hit the ground, the orange bobble on the top began to flash.

"Brilliant," Snowflake beamed, picking up the cone. "It's a light. It will help us see where we're going." He put it back on Wendy's head.

"What's that noise?" asked Wendy.

"What's that smell?" asked Snowflake.

"WITCHES!" they both said at once.

"Quickly," said Wendy, "I don't want them to see me. Hide in the hedge."

The noises got louder and the smell got stronger.

"Ouch! Eek! Mind your elbows. I can't

see where I'm going. I think we're lost," voices whimpered out of the fog. There were horrible sounds of skidding, splintering wood, head-banging, and then a huge thud right in front of Wendy and Snowflake.

A tangle of witches stared at them. Rosemary crawled out of the pile.

"I can see you, Wendy," she snarled. "There's no point trying to hide when you've got a great big flashing light on top of your head."

"You're just jealous," said Wendy, standing up with her hands on her hips. She adjusted her hat so that the orange beam lit up the sky around them. "Soon, everyone will want one of these hats. They are not only stylish but also perfectly practical for a foul, foggy night."

"See and be seen, that's our motto," Snowflake agreed.

He settled down on the back of the broomstick as Wendy climbed on the front.

"It'll take you hours to find your way home in this weather," said Wendy, "so

I wouldn't lie around here if I were you."

Rosemary, Primrose and Harriet were stunned into silence.

Wendy and Snowflake soared skywards, laughing so much that the broomstick rocked backwards and forwards like a see-saw.

Very early next morning a huddle of bruised witches and bandaged cats arrived at Wendy's house.

"Have you still got those lovely red-and-white hats?" called Rosemary.

"Perhaps," replied Snowflake through the keyhole. "Why?"

"We feel it's time for a change," said Harriet.

"Black's a bit boring," said Primrose.

"We'll pay you double," said Rosemary.

"Sold," said Snowflake, whizzing out of the front door and snatching the money. "They're perfect for moonless nights and winter weather. Don't you agree?"

Later, Wendy sat polishing her hat in front of the fire.

"There are a couple of things I don't understand," she said.

"What?" asked Snowflake.

"Firstly, why is our kitchen overflowing with ice-cream cones?"

"They were on special offer," fibbed Snowflake. This was the first time he'd had a go at a spell all on his own. He thought the odd mistake was understandable.

"Don't you think they would make good hats for cats?" mused Wendy.

"Oh, no!" growled Snowflake. "Cat-egorically not. What's the other thing you don't understand?"

"Why did Rosemary, Primrose and Harriet come here for the traffic cones?" asked Wendy. "Why didn't they get them from the side of the road? There must be plenty of them around."

Snowflake rolled his eyes up to the ceiling and leaned hard against the dining room door to try and close it. At the second spelling attempt, Snowflake

had got it right. He'd charmed all the traffic cones in the neighbourhood straight into Wendy's dining room.

"There's something I've been meaning to tell you," Snowflake purred.

But Wendy wasn't listening. She pulled on her hat, switched on the flashing light and waltzed around the room waving her wand.

"Snowflake," she asked, "do you think Rosemary will be a bit nicer to me now?"

"I'm afraid that," giggled Snowflake, "is just witchful thinking!"

Witch★Wendy

BROOM BROOM

Alex Gutteridge

Witch Rosemary's eyes narrowed and turned deep pink, like slivers of beetroot. "Wendy, why are you a walking witch? Where's your broomstick?"

Witch Wendy loves the Annual Broomstick Race – even though she always comes last. But this year she's in big trouble. Her broomstick has broken down – and the Broom Broom Garage can't fix it.

A witch who misses the race faces disaster – and Wendy's cat Snowflake would do ANYTHING to help. But can Wendy be a winner without a zooming broom?